ROAR!

ROAR!

Robert Munsch   **Michael Martchenko**

SCHOLASTIC CANADA LTD.

New York Toronto London Auckland Sydney
Mexico City New Delhi Hong Kong Buenos Aires

The illustrations in this book were painted in watercolour
on Crescent illustration board.
The type is set in 21 point Fairfield.

Scholastic Canada Ltd.
604 King Street West, Toronto, Ontario M5V 1E1, Canada

Scholastic Inc.
557 Broadway, New York, NY 10012, USA

Scholastic Australia Pty Limited
PO Box 579, Gosford, NSW 2250, Australia

Scholastic New Zealand Limited
Private Bag 94407, Botany, Manukau 2163, New Zealand

Scholastic Children's Books
Euston House, 24 Eversholt Street, London NW1 1DB, UK

Library and Archives Canada Cataloguing in Publication

Munsch, Robert N., 1945-
Roar! / Robert Munsch ; illustrated by Michael Martchenko.
ISBN 978-0-545-98020-3
I. Martchenko, Michael II. Title.

PS8576.U575R63 2009   jC813'.54   C2009-902625-2

ISBN-10 0-545-98020-8

6 5 4 3 2 1   Printed in Canada   09 10 11 12

Mixed Sources
Product group from well-managed
forests and other controlled sources
www.fsc.org Cert no. SGS-COC-003098
© 1996 Forest Stewardship Council
FSC

To Isaac and Elena,
Guelph, Ontario
— R.M.

One night, Isaac and Elena read a book about lions.

The next morning, Isaac's mother said, "Good morning, Isaac. Good morning, Elena. Time to get up!"

Isaac said,

"ROAAAAARRRR!"

Elena said,

"ROAAAAARRRR!"

"Oh dear!" said their mom. "What sort of animals are you today?"

"Lions!" said Isaac. "We are lions today."

"Right," said their mom. "My kids are lions."

For breakfast, Isaac and Elena each had a massive, monstrous, meaty bone.

"What's this?" said Elena.

"Lion food," said her mom. "Massive, monstrous, meaty bones make good food for lions."

"Right," said Isaac, and when their mom and dad were not looking, Isaac and Elena gave their bones to the dog.

"ROAAAAARRRR!" said Isaac.

"That was a good bone."

"ROAAAAARRRR!" said Elena.

"That was a good bone."

At school, Isaac's teacher said, "We're going to go for a walk with the Kindergarten. It's SPRINGTIME! Even though our school is in the middle of a city, we are going to find some animals.

"Animals are everywhere!

SHHHHHHHHHHHHHHHHHHHHHHHHHHHHHHH!

Be quiet while we walk."

So the kids and the teacher went out the front door and started to go around the school.

TIP-TOE, TIP-TOE, TIP-TOE, TIP-TOE

After a while Fatima said, "Look, teacher! You're right! There are animals! There is a little baby rabbit right beside the school, a cute baby rabbit hiding in the grass."

All the girls said, "It's so cute! It's so cute! It's so cute!"

Isaac said,

"ROAAAAARRRR!"

The rabbit yelled,

"AHHHHHHHHHHHH!"

and ran away.

WAP – WAP – WAP – WAP – WAP
WAP – WAP – WAP – WAP – WAP

It jumped over the fence and did not come back.

"Isaac!" said his teacher. "DON'T ROAR AT THE ANIMALS!"

Then the kids and the teacher tiptoed very quietly around the school.

TIP-TOE, TIP-TOE, TIP-TOE, TIP-TOE

After a while Paul said, "Look, teacher! You're right! There are animals! There is a little squirrel on the fence. A cute baby squirrel!"

Everyone said, "It's so cute! It's so cute! It's so cute!"

Except Elena! Elena said,

"ROAAAAARRRR!"

The squirrel yelled,

"AHHHHHHHHHHH!"

and ran away.

WAP – WAP – WAP – WAP – WAP
WAP – WAP – WAP – WAP – WAP

It jumped over the fence and did not come back.

"Elena!" said the teacher.
"DON'T ROAR AT THE ANIMALS!"
Then they tiptoed very quietly
around the school.

TIP-TOE, TIP-TOE, TIP-TOE, TIP-TOE

Shakita said, "Oh, teacher! Look!
Coming across the playground is a
mouse, a teeny, tiny, cute little
mouse!"

"AHHHHHHHHHHHHHHHH!"
yelled the teacher. "A MOUSE!
A terrible MOUSE!

"Everybody stand still!"

All the kids stood very, very still.

The mouse came over. It sniffed
Fatima's ear and Shakita's eye and
Elena's arm and Paul's belly button.

But when the mouse came to him, Isaac whispered very softly,

"ROAAAAARRRR!"

The mouse was not frightened. It roared right back at Isaac:

"ROAAAAARRRR!"

"Right," said Isaac. "This mouse thinks it's a lion. On the count of three, EVERYBODY ROAR."

"ONE!

"TWO!

"THREE!

"ROAAAAARRRR!"

The mouse yelled, *"EEEEEEEEK!"*
and ran away.

WAP – WAP – WAP – WAP – WAP
WAP – WAP – WAP – WAP – WAP

It jumped over the fence and did not come back.

The teacher said to ALL the kids,
"DON'T ROAR AT THE ANIMALS!"

"Hey!" said Elena. "Teacher is not an animal. Let's roar at her!"
So all the kids went, "One! Two! Three!

"ROAAAAARRRR!"

And the teacher yelled, **"AHHHHHHHHHHH!"** and ran across the playground.

WAP – WAP – WAP – WAP – WAP
WAP – WAP – WAP – WAP – WAP

She jumped over the fence and did not come back.

Fatima and Elena and Paul and
Isaac ran across the playground.

WAP – WAP – WAP – WAP – WAP
WAP – WAP – WAP – WAP – WAP

They jumped over the fence,
found the mouse hiding under a
leaf, and carried it back to the
classroom.

The whole class was quiet.

"SHHHHHHHHHHHHHHHHHHHHHHH."

And Elena and Isaac got
the mouse on weekends.